OLIVE AND OAK

A GANTON HILLS SHORT

AUBREE PYNN

Edited by
THE EDITING BOUTIQUE

FOREWORD

Special thank you to the tribe. All of you, you know who you are. To my readers, enjoy and thank you for all of your endless support.

Until the end.

This is a short insta-love story that takes place in Ganton Hills.

1

Andru Towns

Freedom felt...bittersweet. It didn't feel like it belonged to me but after seven long years, I finally had it - again. I hadn't seen the sun shine this bright or the stars dancing the way they did, in *seven long years*. Before I got locked up, I was moving more weight than I could keep up with. I was just a street runner that stumbled off the deep-end into some shit. It was all too much too soon; too fast.

Even before then, I never appreciated this shit. The fast life caught up with me. I was constantly looking over my shoulder. Paranoid that either my sins were going to hunt me down or my luck had run out. I can't say they didn't, but I'd be lying if I said that prison didn't save my life.

Unfortunately, I left one hell and swapped it out for another. With my hands shoved into the pockets of my fresh denim jeans, I drifted through what used to be my pop's barbecue joint. This shit used to be popping back in the day. He had everybody and they momma up and through here - gangsta's, sports stars, rappers, and everyone else in between. Now it looked like a bomb had gone off. Technically, it did. A grease fire for insurance purposes and an ego that wouldn't allow him to sell, kept this place in his clutches until his final breath.

The only thing left of it was ashes and a debt.

If I knew *this* was the reason he was holding on to this shit, I would have told him to let it the hell go. I hated the catch, but I understood it. Apparently, the powers that be didn't like when you came up without going through the gatekeeper. Now, the gatekeeper was glaring me in my face. I should have been pissed off but surprisingly, I was cool with this shit.

Up until now, I was trying to keep my nose clean and my head above water. Going back to prison wasn't an option and neither was opening this restaurant without the man himself. The options were few and thanks to pops, the key to forever was three words away.

Nothing in Ganton Hills could open, close, move or enter without permission. I knew pops had ties, but I never expected he was in so deep with this nigga, King. I mean trafficking, cleaning money, serving fiends *deep*. Part of me was ready to walk the fuck out of here, but I knew better.

A heavy sigh left my lips when I was sure I was alone for a second. Standing in the center of the burnt office, I had vivid memories of what it was to grow up here, in this stable. Back then, I remember more good happening here than evil and before I got caught up in street life, I loved being here.

King's heavy footsteps shuffled into the door frame while I was still consumed with my thoughts and dreams of what this was supposed to be when I got out. It was supposed to be, running my pops barbecue joint and elevating this spot. I even hoped to open a few more spots around the city.

The very thing I said I wasn't touching again was going to open the door to so much more. And with the Monarch's protection and no money in my pocket or a decent spot to lay my head, what did I have to lose?

"So, what do you say?" King's heavy commanding baritone forced me to turn around and look him in the eyes like I was taught to do.

I mean shit, I didn't want to do this...but I was already a felon. How long was it going to be until I was right back in my old ways without the hedge?

Before I opened my mouth to speak, I cleared my throat. "I'm with it."

King's eyes danced a bit with acceptance. He didn't reply to me, just whistled - like he was calling a dog. Seven years of prison hadn't softened me in the least. My head was on a swivel. Not knowing who else was in this building with us made me anxious. I spent too much time in solitary for niggas to be rolling up on me like this.

"Dru, what's been up?" The voice was familiar, and it wasn't until I saw his face that fire shot through my veins.

"Nigga, is this a joke?" I asked through gritted teeth staring at Detective Waters.

He chuckled. That was enough for me to run up and steal off on his shit. A few punches and a minor tussle resulted in King's low rumble of laughter followed by, "That's enough."

We went back and forth for another few seconds before I took one more shot at his face.

Detective Waters stepped back and wiped the blood from his lip and nodded, "You got that."

"I know I got it. I ain't that scrawny nigga you locked up seven years ago." I had the height and the muscular weight to handle his ass any day. I'd been thinking about that moment for years and it seemed that this wasn't enough for me. I wanted to kill that nigga.

"Glad y'all met. Hopefully, whatever the beef -"

"Beef? I ain't working with the nigga that busted me. Fucking dirty ass cop," I huffed, washing my face and pacing the floor.

"You want a clean cop on your ass, Dru?" Waters shot back.

Sucking my teeth, I grunted. "Stop sayin' my name! Your crooked ass is probably wired."

Waters laughed and shook his head. "I'm the one keeping all the boys in blue off your ass. Like it or not, I'm your guardian angel."

I shot a look at King only for him to shrug his shoulder. "I honestly don't give a fuck about this lover's quarrel you niggas got going on."

He moved through the office and observed the rummage. "I promised your pops I was going to look out behind you when you got out. The house, the ride, the money, this...I'm looking out. Get this shit up to code in three months so we can get shit movin'. That's when the next big shipment is coming in."

"Oh yeah? How the fuck am I supposed to do that?" I asked as he turned his back.

Waters smirked at me and took a step forward. "Tennessee."

I frowned. "Nigga, you know damn well I can't leave the state."

Water's chuckled and shook his head. "Yeah, I'm aware. She'll be here in a few."

Detective Water's strolled out behind King leaving me with my irritation. Irritation that didn't last long thanks to an alluring, chocolate dipped, thickly stacked mound of God's hand-crafted beauty. I mean seven years without pussy and handling my business with my hand was a lot, and at this point pussy didn't need to have a fine ass face or body to accompany it. I just needed something decent that didn't talk too damn much to allow me to bust a nut and bounce. But this...she...this woman had my body locking up at the sight of her. Not to mention her fucking scent.

Dru don't act like you ain't seen nothing this fine before...

Shit, who was I fooling? I hadn't. I swore she was inching over the debris on the floor in slow motion. Her silk jet black hair moved with her every motion and that saturated copper thigh poked out from the split of her black leather skirt. Every step she took made me want to sink my teeth into her flesh.

If she tasted anything like she looked or smelled, she could be crazy, and I wouldn't mind. Something *that* fine had to be crazy. She looked like she didn't take no shit from anybody, and she was probably carrying some heavy shit most women didn't carry around.

"You sure you can make it through the rest of the building in those heels?"

Man, that's the best you could come up with?

She shot me a glare that was bound to kill. My heart was about to seize up right here and now. They said don't leave the pen and fall in love with the first thing you see. But shit, this woman right here? She was going to be mine without a doubt.

2

Pumae 'Tennessee' Jones

I quickly studied the big man that lurked in the shadows and continued to inch my way through this death trap. When King called me about stocking this place and making sure it was up to code in the next three months, I wasn't expecting this. They were better off burning the rest of it to the ground and cutting their losses.

A few things already had me in a bad mood - my flight delayed in Lavendale, they were notorious for that bullshit, my Uber acted like he couldn't find my hotel, and the rental place was giving me hell about the car I rented. For this reason, exactly, my daddy always taught me to fly private. Next time I was going to take heed to that advice, so much for wanting to be amongst the people and see the sights.

Not to mention, moving through an airport of thousands of people without my piece really had me on high alert. I was six hours removed from the horror of traveling with the rest of the world, and my attitude was shit and dripping off of me.

On top of that, when I walked in here, I was expecting to meet with King, not whoever this man was creeping around the building behind me. After his last comment, he hadn't said anything. Assuming he was kicking himself in the ass for that stupid ass remark, I stepped over a few planks.

His footsteps stopped. I felt him too close for comfort. He had no idea who I was, but I was going to let him find out the hard way. Pulling my gun out my bag I turned it around and pointed it at his head. He had me towered by at least seven inches. For my five-eleven frame to be towered over like this, did something to me.

He wasn't fazed by this. He looked down the barrel and smirked. "How many niggas you shot with this?"

"Several, and I don't mind adding you to the list. Back up you're too close to me," I commented, nudging him with the barrel. He didn't move and if I had to be completely honest it messed with my head for a second.

All he did was lick his full mocha lips, smirked down at me, and extend his hand. "Dru or Big D."

My gun was still pointed as my eyes trailed from his beautiful face to his hand. His nails were manicured, and I didn't spot any dirt but shaking it would mean that I was over myself and I was far from it.

"I'm good," I replied, lowering my gun and putting it back into my purse. "Give me at least six feet of space."

Resuming my life-threatening hike through this mess, I regretted not walking in here in flats. But again, I thought I was meeting King.

"I'm assuming you're Tennessee," he started up again not giving a fuck about my six-foot rule. Dru was trying to get his ass shot. However, I had a funny feeling that bullets didn't scare him.

"I'm assuming they call you Big D..." I tussled my hair, glanced over my shoulder giving him another once over. "Because you're big."

He smirked proudly, "What gave it away? My height?"

"What gave it away? My accent?" I quipped back, and he let out a deep rumble of laughter that sent my body into feeling like I'd been thrown in the fiery pits.

I didn't know who he was, why he was here, or why God was testing my vow to never mess with another man associated with this life. They were either arrogant and couldn't keep their dick in their pants or overcompensating for the ego not worth stroking. Or the ultimate reveal of them not being shit. Niggas weren't shit, period.

Coolly turning around, I sucked in a deep breath. "Well, I've seen enough. I'll tell King to just burn this place to the ground and start over."

I was trying to get the hell out of here without tripping over anything. The last thing I needed after drawing down on him was to trip and put myself in a position to be saved. I didn't need saving, I needed a deep long dick that relaxed my attitude.

Get it together, Pumae.

I needed dinner and sleep. Immediately.

"Whoa, whoa, whoa. Not too fast, Tennessee," he grunted quickening his pace to catch up and grab my wrist.

"I will shoot you, that is a promise, not a threat made by a pretty woman. If you don't let me go I will blow your brains out and burn the building down the rest of the way."

"And you'll tell King what?"

"The truth," I replied. "You seem like you're new around here. Save yourself time and headache and don't ever touch me again."

I didn't want him to relinquish his touch and by the way he debated himself for a few seconds, neither did he. That spark that went off was undeniable. However, I could put on a show and get a daytime Emmy. Every part of me was hoping that his beautiful ass didn't want to force my hand.

Dru slowly released my wrist and stepped back. "This isn't King's place."

My face twisted silently waiting for him to finish that statement.

"It was my pop's. Him and King used to run together. Now it's mine, and I got to get this shit up to code."

I folded my arms over my breasts, blocking his view from my nipples that were starting to perk up, and it wasn't because I was cold. My dumbass decided to wear a lace bra instead of a padded one. Here I was horny and melting off of a deep rumble, enchanting face, and thick ass beard that I could *potentially* soak within seconds.

"Did you hear me?" he rumbled, drawing my attention back to him and off of those full lips and that freshly lined beard.

"Yeah, yeah," I replied with a roll of my wrist. "You need to get this place back up to code. Which means you're one of them."

He frowned. "Meaning?"

"You don't look like a drug dealer," I answered promptly, tussling my hair again.

Okay, Puma cut the bullshit hoe.

His eyes bounced between mine and my erect nipples. Covering them back up quickly, I attempted to pull my gaze await from him while wrinkling my nose. He chuckled lightly before taking a cool stroll around the space. If it were to cool off, I completely understood, I needed to be doused in ice water.

"The goal is to never look like a drug dealer. Expensive ass cars, Armani and Tom Ford suits, and loud ass jewelry only get you caught."

"Spoken like a man that got caught," I muttered, eyeballing his every move until he turned around.

"Yeah, and this is all I got. So, you're either going to help me get this shit together or walk out. Either way, I needed an answer when you walked in."

That was it, I couldn't do this or be around him. His aura alone was going to have me bent over something, shaking and calling him Big D for sure. Ignoring everything in me screaming *run bitch*, I flipped my tresses over my shoulder and said, "it does have good bones. I can start tomorrow."

"That's better," he smoothly replied. "I'll see you tomorrow, Ms. Tennessee."

I snorted with laughter and walked away. Smoothly, confidently, and fast as hell so I could get to my hotel suite and peel myself from these soaked panties. I was going to have to show up tomorrow a little bit more prepared than this.

3

Andru

Baby had my shit on brick and the way her titties were perking up under a niggas glare told me all I needed to know. Most of the night before was fantasizing about what I was going to do to her sexy ass given the opportunity, and a little bit of pressure to make her comply. Appreciating my imagination, I was really tired of that shit though. And I was confident that whatever I envisioned about her would be so farfetched, it would be useless.

It was nine in the morning and she was creeping up the block in her big body Benz. Expecting her to climb out of the car dressed to the nine, I wasn't disappointed. For today, she wore a fitted black dress, a grey GHAMU sweater wrapped around her thick waist showing off the slight pudge, and some black tennis shoes.

I ogled at the stomach though. That let me know that Baby could eat. Just how I liked them. Long legs, thick thighs that could snap my neck and a belly to lay on. I didn't know how long she was here, but it didn't matter because she wasn't leaving.

Tennessee had her hair pulled up into a high bun giving me full access to her round face and cinnamon eyes. Although she looked like she was comfortable today, she didn't spare a detail. She took time in her appearance, another point for her.

Closing the door shut with her hip, she pranced around the car like a damn supermodel holding rolls of paper in her arms. I came to her aid - one because I was raised to be a gentleman and two, that fiery ass attitude I liked. I took them out of her arms without permission.

"I didn't need help," she quipped, locking her rental and strolling into the building behind me.

"I'm a gentleman."

She snorted sarcastically. "A thug and a gentleman, imagine that."

"You soundin' as though you need me to make you a believer."

There went the spark of heat from her again. She attempted to ignore my comment by changing the subject. "Who cleaned up?"

"I did," I proudly announced, putting the rolls of paper on the bar. It was the only stable thing to work from although it was covered in soot. "I'm a hands-on type of man."

"Hmm," she buzzed. "Have you thought about what you want this place to look like?"

I stepped away from her enough for her scent to invade my nostrils and give her enough space to work. "Just like it was with a modern touch."

"You mean a fire hazard?" she asked tooting her red painted lips up and squinted her eyes.

I wasn't supposed to giggle like a fucking school girl but I was caught up and let it flow out like a deep rumble that had Baby gulping. "Nah, it wasn't a hazard until pops set the grease trap on fire."

Her face twisted me. "Interesting. Do you have any pictures?"

I pulled out my phone and fumbled with it a little. Seven years and technology had changed only to fuck with me. The iPhone didn't do all this shit when I had it. There was Airdrop and some other shit. Too cool to tell her I was struggling with this shit, I tried my damndest. She chuckled, slid the phone from between my fingers, and sent the photos to herself.

"How long were you...away?" She didn't give me back her eyes and it was probably best.

I had too many wayward impulses around her ass. I'd mess around and snatch her ass up and get shot. I doubted she would tend to my wounds, so I wasn't trying to test the theory so soon.

"Seven years," I simply replied. "Not counting going in and out for little shit."

"Hmm, it comes with the life I suppose," she muttered looking at the photos. "The cleaning crew will be here in an hour."

She could switch subjects as much as she wanted. I wanted to know more about her. I needed something more to go off of other than she was fine as hell, had a smart ass mouth, and could eat. How did someone like her get wrapped up in a world of gangsta's?

"But what about you? You seem to know your way around this life." Finally, she gave me her eyes accompanied by a smirk that made my heart work double time.

"My daddy and King go back, I assume King goes back with a lot of people. I went to school with his oldest daughter but that's beside the point. My father's company serves only high-end clients of certain backgrounds. I only deal with restaurants that belong to certain clients. It seems you and your guys need extra detail and fine print."

"Hmm," I grunted.

"Uh-huh. This isn't about me though. The cleanup guys will be here in an hour to start gutting this place out. Full construction starts in the morning. I need you to post these permits, so the city doesn't fuck with you, and stay out of the crew's way."

"And where are you going to be?" I asked smoothly, trying to see if she was going to give me something else to chew on.

"Minding the business that pays me. I'll be back in the morning with fixture options. Three months is going to fly by, and I don't want to still be scrambling for shit then, I want to be planning an opening if not already done and enjoying the fruit of my labor."

"It's your world, Baby."

The Baby slipped out, but I was committed to it.

"Tennessee," she corrected, with a glimmer in her eye that made my shit react immediately.

"They're probably a million niggas that call you that, and I'm sure your name ain't really Tennessee so -"

"Please just call me by my name-"

"Your name is Baby until I learn your real name. Ain't no need to fight it, I don't back down easily," I spoke softly but firm enough to make her feel that shit. "Same time tomorrow?"

She chuckled and shook her head. The sweatshirt was keeping me from seeing that ass jiggle as she walked away. "Hang the permits up, Dru. If the city raises hell, it's your ass."

My name sounded so good coming off of her pretty ass lips. I couldn't wait to hear her scream that shit while clawing at my back. Baby let the door close behind her and walked to her car. I watched her get in and pull away. "I sure as hell don't mind you cussing me out."

I hung around and helped the crew finish gutting this place out before I dipped out and headed to mom's spot. Since the will was read, I hadn't had time to get up with her. It was overdue, and I had to get my mind off of Baby and wanting to tear her ass up.

This Range Rover King had delivered at the house in Brentwood was fresh. Black on black, completely murdered out. From the sounds of it, pops stashed the cash left in my old spot after I got locked up. Once I was sentenced he gave it over to King to invest. Everything he'd returned to me was tripled, enough for me to live off of it without ever touching another key. But like everything, that deed came with a price to pay.

Floating downtown with Zaim pumping through my system, I bopped my head to the beat. A few minutes later, I was pulling up to my mom's house. I spent my first three weeks out of the pen here. I loved this woman, but she was smothering me. I mean I got it. She hadn't been able to see her baby boy in seven years. Even at thirty-four, she still had rules for me like I was fourteen.

I was conditioned a certain way. I told myself when I was out I was going to be doing shit at my own pace and time. I had to take what I had in my pocket when they arrested me and find what I could. Although my Brentwood spot was an upgrade from the ran down apartment I rented, the apartment was something I did on my own. I had pride about that shit.

Swinging my long legs out of the truck, I grabbed my duffle bag off the back seat, secured the door, and strolled up to the screen door. The front door was wide open, she must have been waiting on someone else to swing by. As I pulled the screen door open I was greeted with the smell of something good.

"You must have known I was coming," I spoke up announcing myself so her crazy ass didn't draw down on me.

Moms was a gangsta, it was my pops that was straight until he got caught up with her. Legend has it moms and pops ran heavy with King back in the day, before and after Prophete got killed. I never really went into detail with them about it. They both hated talking about that night. According to the vague details they shared every so often, nothing was the same after Prophete was murdered. 'Til this day, Ganton Hills was still feeling the effect of an OG getting slain by the niggas he called brothers.

For that reason, I moved by myself. I didn't like the idea of Waters being involved with shit I had going on. I was going to test that nigga though. I wasn't a snitch, but if that nigga thought I was going this time without setting this city on fire, he was wrong.

"Your sister is bringing the baby by and this food is for Ms. Wilson up the street. I figured y'all talked so I made enough," she shared from the kitchen. "I ain't seen you in a minute."

I stepped into the guest bathroom to wash the dirt and sweat off of me and changed into some grey sweatpants and a fresh t-shirt and a pair of Jordan's. My past taught me to never leave the house without a fresh outfit packed away. Anything could happen that called for a quick switch.

"Don't act like you miss me," I called from the bathroom.

Being sure to clean up behind myself, I walked out of the bathroom and dropped my bag by the front door.

"I do miss you," she admitted. "I also understand that you are a grown ass man and you need your space to run your hoes in and out of."

I scoffed in laughter as I lowered myself into a seat at the table. "I'm chilling ma."

She mimicked my scoff and shot me a glance. "Tell me prison ain't...changed you."

"Go play with someone else," I huffed, waving her off. "Pussy will always be pussy, and can't no nigga take that from me. You also forget I spent most of my time in solitary. Nobody wanted to fuck with the crazy nigga."

She chuckled. "Touché. How are you handling this transition?"

I shrugged. "I'm cool. You know me, I could always adjust to shit. If that didn't break me ain't shit going to."

"Just like your daddy."

I considered that a compliment even though that nigga was stubborn as hell.

4

Pumae

I spent all day ordering, buying, and confirming measurements for the restaurant. I was consumed with this project. If I could cut the timeframe down, I was going to do that. I *needed* to do that. Every moment I spent in that man's presence felt like I was suffocating while being set on fire. I didn't like it, but I was craving that shit. I couldn't understand why my body was betraying me like this.

"Have you seen King yet?" daddy asked.

"Not yet, I'm supposed to meet up with him tomorrow, though. You know God daddy, never in one place too long. By the time I got to the spot yesterday he was already gone."

Daddy laughed a little. "Nah, he could never stay still. How is everything else? You miss being home?"

The truth was, nothing felt like home the way Ganton Hills did. I spent my formative years here, I went to college here. It wasn't until mom passed and dad retired that we left. I felt her here, and I didn't want to leave. But staying here meant a lot more trouble than the agony of missing her.

I sighed and pulled into the parking lot of Juicy Lucy's. I'd been yearning for a double cheeseburger, their seasoned fries, and a peach shake since I touched down. This is why I was this size now. I spent all four years of college in Juicy Lucy's. Now, at thirty-two, I couldn't get rid of this pudge and hips if I ate air for a year straight.

"I miss you, if that's what you mean," I spoke up killing my engine. "But you know I love Ganton Hills."

"Don't I know it, King called, and you were on the first thing smoking, you couldn't even wait for me to gas up the jet," he said with a laugh. "I won't rush you home, but please be back for my birthday."

"When have I ever missed a birthday?" I asked, climbing out the rental and shutting the door. "I will be there with bells on."

Locking the car, I walked into the burger shop and stood in line. "What have you been doing without me?"

"The same thing I do every day, golf, shoot the shit and count my money," he shared with a laugh.

I couldn't help but laugh. "You and your love for money."

"That's why you should keep luring these clients in and charging them top dollar."

"I know, I do what I can."

My body was reacting again. The hairs on my neck were standing at attention and I was on fire. That was just from a thought of Dru. The mere thought of that fine ass man littered in tattoos, eyes that saw some shit, and soul housed in a cage of a man that wanted to be free, had every muscle in my core tight.

"I knew you had other niggas calling you," his voice rumbled in my ear. I quickly spun around with my jaw dropped. Snapping my mouth shut the second he smiled down at me, I pulled myself back together.

"Daddy," I hummed as sweetly as I could. "I'll call you back later."

"Alright, Mae. I love you."

"Love you too, daddy." I hung up and looked Dru over.

Simple grey sweats that told on him, they almost made me bite my lip, and a crisp white tee that hugged his muscular chest. They didn't call him Big D because of his height, they called him Big D because of that weight. I really didn't need to slip and fall around him.

"And you call him daddy too," he groaned, gripping his chest like I did some damage.

"Because he's my father, fool." I didn't want to laugh but it just came out. "Are you always so…"

"Forward with what I want? Yeah," he replied, looking me over.

I needed him to stop that shit.

It took every single ounce of sense in my body to turn me back around. I wasn't a weak bitch but Dru was a fight of unseen proportion for my guard.

I went through all of that to turn back around and say, "Dru I am not to be fucked with. You should stop while you're ahead."

He licked his lips and I thought about how that principle of lust and whatever else he was capable of, would feel as I dragged myself over it.

"You're up." He nodded his head. "We got a line behind us, Baby."

Move your feet, Pumae.

Dru was finding pleasure in the fact that he had my ass stuck like this. I mean frozen. I didn't like it, I fucking hated it! Dru wrapped his hand around my waist so he could spin me around and lead me to the counter. He leaned on it and chuckled to himself.

"What are you getting?" he asked, locking eyes with me.

I pulled my orbs away and cleared my throat. "Can I get a double cheeseburger, large fry, and a peach milkshake, please. And a cup of special sauce on the side."

"Anything else?" he inquired.

"A bottle of water." I turned my head to dig into my purse for my wallet.

Gently sliding me out of the way, he ordered and paid for the food. So, what it was twenty bucks, I was going to give it back off principle.

"Find a spot where I can see the door," he commanded softly.

"I was taking this to go," I quipped only for him to smile.

How in the hell were his teeth this white after seven years in prison?

"Baby." He stood up straight and looked down at me. "Find a booth."

My damn feet were betraying me. They just took off to find a table. I worked too hard for my independence, and not to be someone's trophy. Dru would have my ass prancing around his house with a feather duster butt ass naked.

Sliding into the hard booth I smoothed the back of my hair and considered sliding out of here. Of course, my body was stuck.

Of course, I couldn't move.

Of course, I wanted to succumb. My body knew it was in the presence of a real nigga, no matter how hard I tried to fight it.

When he sat down, I handed him the twenty and he laughed. "Go play with someone else. If I wanted the money back, we wouldn't be sitting here. Why have you been paying for your shit when there's a man present?"

"I was raised to be independent and not depend on a man for anything." What the hell was I saying? I wanted to depend on him for a nut in his world or five, whichever came first. I left the money on the table and looked at him in the face. "Nothing is ever free."

"Depending on a man ain't a bad thing," he commented. "You only held onto that because you've never been in the presence of a real one. That's about to change though."

He peeled the paper off of my straw and stuck it into my milkshake and winked. "But I assure you, I'll take good care of you."

"Is it crack you're smoking?" I asked with a laugh. "It's got to be."

"Nah," he responded before dropping his head. "Bless this food, amen."

"Amen."

"And it ain't crack, Baby. I'm a grown ass man. I know what I want."

5

Andru

In order to be a business owner, I needed to look like a business owner. I was cool with these tee's, sweats, and jeans on a day to day. I hadn't worn shit else in seven years, but I needed to switch it up. A tailored suit in the three colors I needed was enough to get me by for the time being. Nothing too flashy to get eyes on me. I learned my lesson, and I wasn't trying to have a repeat of it, just what I needed. Plus, King wanted me to meet him at this upscale spot that required me to look like money, as he put it.

I ran my hand down the tie and glanced over my shoulder at my older sister bouncing her daughter in her arms. Since I'd been home she'd pop up randomly to make sure I was cool. It didn't matter how old we were, she still needed to feel needed. I was cool with it. My circle had dwindled down to just her and moms.

"Don't look at me for assurance. You know you're fine. You're trying to catch some hoes. I hope you're wrapping it up."

I chuckled, dusted my shoulder off, and walked out of the walk-in closet. "Nah, no hoes."

"Dru," she sounded off like she didn't believe me. Ryan was never a person not to believe any of my farfetched stories, why she was acting like this was extreme was beyond me. "Don't tell me no shit like you fell in love or anything like that."

I didn't say shit, I just laughed to myself and grabbed my keys. The mere thought of Tennessee would have me stuck.

"Nah, Dru. Don't do that and try to stroll out of here like it's cool."

"I'm not calling it love, but she's mine, ain't a question about it."

"And how do you know this?"

"A man knows what he wants. Boys play games," I answered watching her squint her eyes.

Ryan pressed her lips together and hummed. "Mmhmm, you didn't have to read me like that. Who is she, anyway?"

"I didn't read you," I corrected. "I just know you deserve better than that nigga you with. And why would I tell your nosey ass that? So, you can stalk her crazy ass? I think not."

"You like them crazy types. Don't get your ass caught up."

I waved her off. "You and moms are live wires. Where do you think I get the taste of crazy from?"

"Whatever, you're going to be late. I'm going to figure out who she is, watch."

"Don't get too close to her, she's strapped," I added before walking out the house. "Lock up!"

King didn't play about time, I sped to the spot I was meeting him and valeted. When I walked in I was escorted to a private dining room. I wasn't expecting to see him and David, but it didn't matter, I was always prepared for whatever. A quick pat down by his security, I shook their hands and took a seat.

"We're expecting one more," King spoke up just as the door opened again.

Tennessee walked in, clad in an olive hued dress that hugged every damn curve she had. Her curled hair fell over her shoulders and bounced with every step. To me, she was moving in slow motion and my body was reacting to her. Pulse quickening, breathing stopped, dick doing somersaults and shit. I caught her eye for a moment before she looked away and smiled at King.

"Hey, God daddy." Her voice was full of joy as she hugged King and then David. "Hey, Uncle David. I wasn't expecting a party."

"You and Andru already met, it was easier to meet with both of you about the renovations of the restaurant."

Disappointment flashed on her face for a second. "And here I was thinking it was just a free meal."

King chuckled and flashed his goddaughter a look. "You know I always take care of you, but business never sleeps."

"I've fast tracked the permits to the restaurant and the timeline. The shipment is coming in a few weeks and it's going to be stored at the restaurant," David spoke up diving right into the business. "Pumae, you're going to make sure the liquor closet has a faux wall and a hollow spot for the product."

"The contractors called to let me know that back rooms are ready for whatever in a few days. Most of the work is going to be the kitchen and the dining room, so that's going to be easy. We'll be ready. I've also included floor safes in the renovations to the back offices. There is an exit in Dru's office that leads straight to the alley," she proudly shared with the room.

Fine as fuck. *Check.*

Had a good appetite on her. *Check.*

Smart as a whip. *Check.*

Was she a rider though? That was the pressing question.

"Well, that was easy. I'm sure you'll walk Dru through everything," King spoke up before his phone rang. Excusing himself, he walked away to handle his phone call. David was consumed by his own phone. I was going to allow Pumae this time to pretend I hadn't been keeping her up at night like she'd been keeping me.

A few minutes later, King hastily walked back in, he gave David a look that prompted him to get up.

"We have some shit to handle. The tab is taken care of. Stay and eat," King spoke, kissing Pumae's cheek. "I'll reschedule our dinner. Promise."

Pumae smiled faintly as they whisked out the back door.

"I'm going to go ahead and -" she started gathering her things.

"Sit down, Baby."

She squirmed a bit but didn't get up. Her melanin deepened under my glare. I loved that shit. Imagining how many shades she'd turned when I filled her gut up was a delight. "I'm not leaving because I'm hungry."

"Whatever you tell yourself, *Pumae*."

That heat from her spiked and the blood was rushing from my head. "Tennessee."

"Now that I know your real name, I ain't coming off of it, Baby. And that shit is sexy too."

"I'm aware. My mother…" she started then stopped. "She said I came in the middle of the night, with an incredible strength and the beauty of a puma."

"She didn't lie," I responded, studying her.

"Don't look at me like that please," she let out just above a whisper. "I don't ask for anything, but I really need you to stop looking at me like that."

The heat and sexual tension were rising in this room and if it was broken soon I was going to tear that dress off of her and devour her. Tugging at my tie, the waitress showed up just in time. She took our orders and was sure to pay extra attention to mine. I could see Pumae's smolder from the corner of my eye. It was only a matter of time before she dropped this act. It wasn't until the waitress left that she made a smart ass comment.

"You need me to excuse myself so she can continue?"

A low roar of laughter escaped my mouth. "I don't need her to do shit for me."

"Mm, but she'll be willing to do whatever."

"She's a pick me. You have to watch people who don't require shit from you before handing themselves over. It's the people that give you some push back that are worth having. It's the fight I want. The woman who has her own shit that wants nothing from me but love, respect, and soul snatching attention. The woman who requires me to be the best man I can and pushes and protects my spirit. I want the woman with stability. Quickie pussy don't mean shit to me, I spent seven years without it, what's another few -"

"Another few what? You think that you're going to break me down and walk off with my pussy?" she asked in amusement. "I don't think so."

"I'm already breaking you down," I shot back, sitting back. "You just got to shoot the shot."

She curled her lip and shook her head. "I swear men always have the audacity."

"I've always been a bold type. I see what I want, I go and get it. I ain't never had nothing I didn't take care of. But I get it, you have a job to do. I ain't about to complicate your shit, just know it's over."

She scoffed and rolled her eyes. "Alright, Andru."

I licked my lips and glared at her. She wasn't going to let me in so easily, she glared back at me. "Pumae, baby the longer you fight what you feel, the longer it's going to take you to get your blessing."

The waitress was timely with returning with the drinks and the food. Pumae didn't say much of anything else, outside of answering a few questions. She drank and ate until she saw a window to escape out of. I wasn't ready for her to leave my presence. It was very clear she hadn't ever dealt with a nigga that was going to be all she needed.

She'd been picking up the slack, packing bags, and hoarding them in the closet. Talking herself out of what she really wanted for the sake of being guarded and protected, was coming to an end. She'd only been this way because she didn't have anyone outside of King and her people to do it.

There was room for her here. I went through seven years of cleaning and ridding myself of shit, unknown of the reason. Now the reason was a few feet away from me, waiting on an Uber to take her back to her hotel.

"Why didn't you drive?" I coolly asked.

"I don't like driving in the dark," she simply replied.

"Let me take you to your spot," I said as the valet pulled my whip around.

She shook her head no. "So, you can weasel your way upstairs to check behind the curtains?"

"Baby, you're too damn smart to fall for the oldest trick in the book. Lucky for you I don't play games and I ain't on no funny shit. I ain't attacking your fine ass until you say go. Feel me?"

Pumae shot me a look at the corner of her eye like she was going to give the go ahead now. If that were the case I wouldn't have taken the leap. I was a heavy nigga, I came with shit she wasn't ready for and after four drinks she didn't need to make any heavy decisions on a whim.

I opened the passenger door for her and waited until she pranced over and climbed in. Rounding the truck, I folded myself in and headed toward the hotel. The chiming of her phone kept her occupied for a few minutes.

"Shit," she hissed, hitting a combination of icons on her screen.

Looking over my shoulder, I took in how good she looked riding shotgun. "Everything good?"

"No, the contractors didn't set the alarm for the restaurant," she groaned. "Something is tripping the back door."

"Aight," I buzzed, hitting a U-turn in the intersection and speeding up toward the restaurant.

"It's probably a cat or something."

"Either way, it needs to be taken care of right?"

She smirked a bit. "Yeah."

"And I want to see what you've done so far. Kill two birds with one stone."

"White walls and plastic tarps aren't much to see."

"But it's better than what was there before."

Pulling up to the restaurant, I directed her to stay where she was until I checked out the building. Cautiously entering the building with my gun drawn, I reached for the light switch and stepped over some shelves lying on the floor. Of course, she didn't listen, she was strutting in right behind me with her gun out.

"What part of *stay in the car* did you miss?" I threw over my shoulder.

"Uh the part about you being a convicted felon," she said with a huff. "Put your gun away. You're not even supposed to have that."

"Let me find out you care."

"Not the time for your jokes, Andru."

With her gun in her right hand and her purse in the left, she sashayed her sexy ass past me and checked the back door. I went to check the rest of the doors and met her in the back hall. Being that we were busy securing the building I wasn't going to make the comment about how good she looked in that dress, holding that gun and smelling like she was ready for the eating. I was going to admire it and take a mental snapshot.

She pushed her hair out her face and muttered, "Dumbasses didn't lock it."

She groaned to herself, secured the door, and left me in the back by the offices. Pop's office was gutted, cleaned, and repainted. Plastic was taped on the wall to keep the dust off of them until the floors were done.

Remembering how this space looked before I was eager to make it my own. Roaming from the offices to the gutted out kitchen to the bar area, it was looking like something again. Pumae was good at what she did. The amount of planning and execution it took to restore a building this fast amazed me.

"No, I don't need an officer to show up, it was just the back door. It's fine," I heard her say. "Please don't send them."

Finding her standing in the liquor closet, Pumae was staring at three bricks with her free hand buried in her hair. While trying to convince the security company that she was fine, she shot me a look. I read her expression and turned to the parchment paper covered windows.

I could hear the sirens in the distance. Pumae wasted no time dropping the bricks in her purse and zipping it shut. As she stepped out I pulled the shelf in front of the space and pulled the door shut. Whatever was going to happen next, I needed to be calm.

She was fuming, though. I didn't know how her temper was set up. She could have popped off the mouth the moment the officers knocked, or she could play this shit cool as a fan. I was interested on top of finding that scowl to be sexy as fuck.

One thing was for sure we were going to figure this shit out after this was over. Leaving her bag on the counter she turned her charm on and walked to the door. "Stay cool."

I stood in the middle of the room with my hands in my tailored pants and watched her work all of that shit she carried. Pumae pulled the door open and tousled her hair to the side. "Officers."

"We got a call about the alarm." I heard Detective Waters and immediately got pissed.

I could see her body language shift, but her tone remained even.

"They sent a detective to come and check out an alarm?" she asked. "Well, it's just Andru and me, and we were just leaving."

"Where y'all headed to?" he asked. "We need to clear the building."

"Now, Detective, your only concern should be the alarm. Or is there something else you left behind?" she quizzed blocking his view into the building and me. "Something else you need? Or are we good?"

"We're good. I'll let them know everything is good. You should be careful, the alley is dangerous at night."

"I imagine the daylight is just as dangerous for a rat," she shot back.

They knew each other far more than acquaintances. By the way her shoulders were squared, she couldn't stand the nigga. That made two of us.

"I'll be seeing you."

"You will."

Pumae waited until he cleared the officers before shutting the door and locking it. "Your partner is shady as they come."

"He's a bitch," I replied, stepping to her. "You good?"

She nodded. I didn't know everything about her, but I was learning by the second. She had a way of handling shit quickly. The way she stuffed those bricks in her bag without hesitation told me all I needed to know. Baby checked every box. Her actions only reaffirmed that she was the one.

"You sure?"

"I'm good Dru, just give me a minute."

She moved from me grudgingly to her bag and grabbed her phone. I could hear the line ring a bit before whoever she called picked up.

"My fingerprints are all over this shit. The next time there's an emergency and someone needs to stash some shit, I'd like a heads up...no, he just left...tell his stupid ass to meet me at the back door his dumbass left unlocked and opened...and God daddy, you should really consider getting rid of him."

Pumae hung up and motioned me over. She was still in go mode. As she pulled the pocket square from my jacket, I could feel the anxiety bouncing off of her. Carefully removing the bricks from her purse, she wiped them off with my pocket square and dropped them in a box. I knew when to step up and to fall back. This was her show and I was getting a front row seat.

I kept a close eye on her as she went to the back door and pushed the box into Waters' chest. "Pull some shit like that again and you're going to have more than my attitude to deal with. I don't like being put into positions because you're fucking stupid."

"Is that any way to talk to you-"

"Nigga, shut up," she groaned slamming the door shut.

"Let me find out that's your ex," I teased as she walked past me.

"Sophomore to junior year, I don't count him as a body. He's a bitch. I'm ready to go."

My shit was harder than concrete. She had made the last fifteen minutes extremely hard for me. As she walked over to the wall where the alarm was located, I caught her by the wrist and pulled her into my body. "Why did you do that?"

Pumae tried to block my gaze into her soul by looking away. Gently pulling her chin back center, I asked again. "Why did you do that?"

"I didn't feel right letting you go down for some bullshit. Waters is a bit-"

I cut her off with an impulsive kiss. I'd been wanting to do this shit. A soft peck quickly led to our tongues wrestling, light moans exchanged, and my hand squeezing the base of her neck. Judging by the heat escaping her pores, she liked that shit. My free hand gripped her waist then her ass. Pumae's light moan turned into a purr. Lost in the sauce of this, I had her pinned between the wall and my body, hiking her thigh up.

"Fuck," I grunted, pressing my forehead against hers and pulling my hands from her body. "I said I wasn't doing this shit yet. Let me take you home."

I willed myself away from her and let her punch the code in. After I secured the building, I got in the car and looked at her. Pumae's purse was in her lap, she crossed her ankles and locked her fingers. Closing herself off to me was the best option or else we would have been seeing what kind of shocks this Range had.

We rode in silence for almost ten minutes until I broke it, I couldn't take it. I needed to hear her voice. I found it crazy as hell that in a few days, I was hooked like this to a woman I just met. I was never a man to question God's timing. He deserved some praise for this. For this, I was considering meeting moms at church.

"You sure you good, though?"

She sighed faintly and took her attention from the city lights to give it to me. "Look, I was raised by gangster's, but I don't like getting my hands dirty. Or being put into situations, by anyone. That shit was foul. He could have stashed the shit anywhere, but he knew…"

She took a deep breath and pushed her head into the headrest. "Now, I remember why I haven't come back home."

"You let a nigga run you away from your home?" That was unsettling to me and I felt the need to protect her from that.

She gave me the softest look and my chest tightened. A shift had happened that fast, walls down for a moment. "I'm not proud of that."

"Makes sense, though," I mumbled. "He doesn't represent all of us. And he sure as hell ain't shit to be trippin' over."

"You're right."

"Can you say that again, that shit felt good."

"Hold on to it, that's the only feeling you're going to get."

I scoffed. "Too late, Baby."

After dropping her off and ensuring she made it safely inside, I strolled back to my car only to be met by Waters and that stupid ass look on his face. I didn't want shit to do with him, let alone work with this shady nigga. I felt like King was testing me - trying to see if I was going to roll over or not.

"Are you enjoying my damaged goods?" Waters asked. "You know her ass is crazy and uncooperative right?"

He was testing my patience, but he didn't understand that seven years of hell made me a very patient man. He was going to get his ass caught up in some shit before I could even reach out to touch him. While he was concerned about comparing dick sizes, I was focused on the future and everything it held. Unfortunately for him, it meant, Pumae at my side.

"Sounds like you lack the fundamental skills it takes to handle a grown ass woman," I commented, stopping a few feet short of him. "Do you have some real business to talk to me about or you here to put your dick on the table?"

I'd already wrecked his shit once, I didn't want to do it again on the street.

My freedom came with the cost of not letting my temper have its way.

"I actually came to talk to Tennessee."

"Tennessee, huh? The damaged goods that's uncooperative and crazy?" I asked. I scoffed to myself as I sized him up. Square ass nigga looking for validation in an underworld he couldn't successfully hold his weight. I was convinced now more than ever that King only brought him around to weed out his bitchassness. "She's good and has probably had enough of you for this lifetime. Now if you don't mind."

He stepped closer, Waters was trying to taunt me. Badge or no badge, if Waters didn't tread lightly it would be his ass would be the one locked up in a pen like a fucking animal.

"You should watch how you move around my city. This shit you got with Tennessee is going to be short lived."

"Your city?" Laughing and stepping around his ass, I shook my head. "Detective, you only have a few hours left of night crawling. Do it from around me and mine."

6

Pumae

I'd been staying clear of Andru for the last two weeks. I had to. My wall dropped and it would only lead me to poor decisions and being pinned up in his bed. Or worse trying to get his imprint and scent off of me. I wasn't going back to being that woman. After he kissed me like that, I lost sleep; started looking up his address like a crazy woman so I could Uber to his spot and get some more.

I needed more and that was dangerous. Andru was the type to get me so caught up in him I would lose my mind. I wasn't getting stupid over a man again. I said that, but everything about Andru felt right, though.

The last contractor was packing up his things while I scrolled through my phone checking the status of a few orders yet to arrive. When they all left, I moved from my workspace in the corner to the bar.

Not willing to sit down until I walked through the building with my checklist. The only things that needed to go up were the final fixture, some kitchen equipment, and the liquor my people were delivering in the morning.

Rounding back to the bar, I rubbed my neck and groaned. Plopping down on the barstool, I sighed tiredly. I'd been in and out of here all day. A hot shower and a bottle of wine were calling my name.

The door opened and just like that his scent had my walls down and sense fleeting. "Glad I showed up. You were just going to sit in here all night with the door unlocked?"

As happy as I was to be in his presence, I was trying to play this coolly. I really wanted to skip my sore body over to him and engulf him in a hug. "I was going to get it."

He gave me a lopsided grin and shook his head. "Heard you haven't eaten all day."

I stared up at him casually dressed and still fine as hell. "They work for me, they aren't supposed to be snitching on me."

"They know who the real boss is. And it's also eleven at night. You were going to drive?"

"I was going to call an Uber."

"Here I am," he replied with that damn smile.

I liked him. Maybe it was the fact that he wasn't trying to be someone else. Just him. He was forceful enough but hadn't invaded my space. Which was the only reason he didn't have a collection of my panties yet. I was never one to shoot my shot. I didn't take rejection well, I just pulled triggers.

I laughed and took a deep breath. "Are you ready for the tasting tomorrow night? This place is going to be complete by noon."

"That's really why I'm here," he spoke up, holding the bags up. "Getting some stuff prepped for tomorrow. You sliding out on me or do you want to stay to learn a little something?"

"What are you teaching?" I asked with a lick of my lips. That was the wrong move for me and my guard. Andru invaded my space without permission, gently kissed my lips, and stepped back.

"Tennessee heat and a homemade rub. Are you trying to learn or what?"

I would be lying if I said I packed my shit up and went back to my hotel. My hungry, greedy for dick and attention, ass was plopped right on the stainless steel counter watching his fine ass whip up a small dish of grits, bacon, and shrimp.

It was something about watching this man cook that had me rethinking my life of forever lonely. He was focused on what he was doing but still attentive to me.

"Have you thought about the name yet? Are you going to keep it the same?"

"I mean Big L's is cool, but Olive and Oak has been sticking out," he replied.

His muscles flexed while he plated the shrimp and grits with a few slices of smoked brisket.

"At the corner of Olive Boulevard and Oak Haven, I like it."

His smile beamed as he spun around and stood between my thighs. "Yeah, that's it. Hearing it off your lips is confirmation."

Too close, too fine, and far too much heat. My stomach was doing somersaults. My heart was about to explode out of my chest. If Andru didn't move, this kitchen was going to see something it never saw before.

"Open up," Andru commanded so softly that I was willing to hold my legs open while he fed me, deeply pulling sounds out of me I hadn't heard...ever. What type of shit was this?

Keeping my eyes on his, I opened my mouth and let him feed me. He was different. A rare find that I would probably never encounter again. Everything melted in my mouth while I melted from my center. At that moment, my mind was made up, he could have some pussy tonight.

"Who taught you how to cook like this?" I asked, covering my mouth still trying to savor the flavor.

"My pops. He wasn't a gangsta. Not like moms. She's hardcore with a gentle soul. She says I'm like him and he said I was like her. Anyway, he cooked everything all the time. This block used to be jumping."

"Tell me he passed along his smoked rib recipe."

"Baby, I got everything. Give a nigga a shot, you'll eat forever."

I gulped and grabbed a bottle of water off the counter. Chugging it down to reset my nerves, he laughed and pulled it from my lips. Andru's massive hand cupped my face and his thumb traced my lips. "What are you so afraid of, Pumae?"

My eyes fluttered. The possession of my face in his hand wouldn't allow me to pull away.

"Hm?" he nudged me gently for an answer.

"You," I answered simply.

I was so tough on the outside. Such a bad bitch, but this bad bitch needed tender love and care. I longed for someone to call home, I wasn't cut out to be alone no matter how good I made it look. And Andru - Andru felt so safe and secure. He would be the perfect place for me to lay down my sword.

Andru took custody of my lips. He wasn't in a rush and I loved that. It was tantalizing when shit was done slow and easy with a touch of aggression no matter how much shit I talked. "You ain't got shit to be afraid of, Baby."

My hands found the side of his beautiful face. "Why do I trust you like this?"

"It came naturally. I wasn't looking to be wide open behind you, but I can't help myself."

Allowing my fingers to stroke his beard, I took it a step further and let myself surrender to this moment, to this feeling. Our lips collided again, and the heat only intensified. His hands were exploring my body and my curves were ready for his expedition. I was just trying to hold on for the adventure. His hand slid into my leggings and pulled my panties to the side.

The touch of my wetness against his fingers caused him to hiss. "You've been keeping this from me? Take this shit off."

Dipping his middle finger between my folds forced me to gasp and arch my back.

"Shhh," I shuddered, rising up so he could pull my legging and panties off. My sandals fell off my feet as he pushed my legs up and dived in head first.

"Mm," I moaned, melting under his touch.

He hungrily rolled his tongue over my center with an unmatched suction, I was going to cum without warning. I thought this shit was bound to make me crazy until he came up inserted his finger inside. Dru pressed on my g-spot and my clit at the same time. That was going to cause him some trouble. She wasn't going to forget that.

Trying to grip the counter, I knocked a few dishes over.

"Open your eyes," he growled. "When I give you this dick, ain't no turning back. You understand?"

This was unfair. He couldn't talk shit like this while massaging my g-spot and clit at the same time. I was shivering and searching for words I didn't have.

"Pumae," he growled. "You understand?"

I nodded.

His pressure didn't let up. A sloppy kiss was placed on my lips. "Use your words."

"I-I understand, Dru. I hear you, shit. This isn't fair. You-you can't do this to me here, like this."

He smirked, slid his fingers out, and sucked my juices from them. "You're right. I need more space. Let's clean up so I can take you home."

"Huh?" I asked. "Home?"

"Yeah, where you should have been the second I laid eyes on you."

7

Andru

We cleaned up, locked up, and were in transit to my spot. This shit was wild. Everything felt right, I didn't care about a timeline or what anyone would say. Pumae gave me the ball and I wasn't missing shots or fumbling. She wasn't the type I could play with. I would be dead by the time the thought crossed my mind.

Pulling into the garage, I killed the engine and looked over at her. "You good?"

She smiled, brightly and beautifully. "I am."

Swinging my legs out I rounded the car while the garage door closed and opened her door. "Welcome to my humble home."

"Definitely has my spot beat," she replied. Taking her hand in mine, I led her inside. "For sure, you got me beat."

I laughed. "I'll grow into it. You know, kids, a dog or two."

"You want kids?" she asked like it was a shock.

I turned to her. "Don't you."

"Never thought I would have any, honestly. You know, a woman hits thirty with no prospects she's kind of just thrown away. But thirty-two and the only man you have is your daddy, shit gets bleak."

A confident smirk crossed my lips. "God was just saving you for me is all."

"You're mighty confident."

I invaded her space and kissed her. "Damn right. You want something to drink?"

"I can drink later," she mumbled against my lips.

"Point of no return, Pumae." I was giving her one last chance to change her mind.

She chortled and started up the stairs and stopped halfway to look down at me. "Dru, you'll learn one thing about me. She doesn't like to wait. Ever."

Sprinting up the stairs, I picked her up and wasted no more time. Pumae ripped my shirt from my body, impatiently waiting for my lion to tame her puma. Holding her close, I tore her leggings off and stepped away.

It was like a tug of war. I wanted to admire how beautiful she was while getting her naked and feeling her flesh pressed against mine. Lust flooded her eyes, and she pulled her shirt over her head and tossed it to the floor.

"You are fucking beautiful."

Not wasting another second, I attacked her flesh where she stood. From her lips to her toes and everything in between. Pumae looked good and tasted even better. She wasn't getting rid of me, I would scorch the earth to protect her and to keep her here. Hoisting her thick body on my shoulders, I sucked her juices from her center before dropping her on the bed.

Naked with her guard down was how I wanted to keep her. Stepping out of my sweats and my boxers, I loved the look in her eyes while my dick bounced from side to side. She clamped down on her lip and ran her hand down to her center. The view from here made my dick jump.

I drifted to my top drawer and opened the box of condoms. Ripping one open and rolling it down my shaft, I walked over to the bed where she was putting in work without me.

"Nah, you don't get to cum without me, Baby."

She yelped as I pulled her to the edge of the bed by her ankles. I used the back of my hand to knock hers out the way and took control of her pussy with my lips.

Her purrs, moans, and directions filled the room. Pumae pushed my head deeper into her mound, juices covered my nose and dripped down my beard. I smacked and grunted into my full spread. Slurping up every drop, nothing was going to get by me. Happy I waited for some quality shit instead of diving into the first piece of pussy I crossed. This was A1. Groomed, tended to, pH balanced shit. You knew how much a woman took care of herself by this.

She locked her legs around my neck. That's that shit I liked - feeling like I could die with my face submerged in her ocean. This was heaven on earth. The land of honey between these thick, buttery thighs. The more she shook, the tighter her legs wrapped around my neck. The tighter the grip, the louder the moans. I waited until her moans went silent to pull myself out her hold.

"You are talented," she purred as she gleaned up at me. Pumae had me feeling like the king of the world.

Parting her legs open wider and pressing my head at her opening, I grunted, "don't fucking run."

I pushed inside of her slowly, filling her up and enjoying her entire body change shades. Her pretty face contorted through expressions. "Ahh, shit."

Her spine arched to the ceiling, and her hands pressed against my hips to control my strokes. They were quickly moved, wrapped up in mine, and pinned over her head. All she did was force me to grind deeper inside. Pumae's breathing hitched and her pussy quivered.

"Gahhhhdamnnn," she gasped. "Don't fuckin' stop, daddy."

"Take your dick like a champ." Every pump inside felt like I was going home. Her body was designed for me. She adjusted and pulled me closer.

"You feel like home, Baby," I grunted in her ear.

Between moans and clawing at my back when I let her wrists go, she hummed in my ear. "So, do you. Please don't fuck this up. Handle me with care."

I did. Shit, I gave her all I had. Deep, fast, slow, steady. Everything she needed, however, she needed it done. It wasn't about me, this was about us tying a knot that was never going to be untied.

Pumae used her thick thighs to flip me over on my back. Taking me all the way in she rolled her hips and slid down my shit, peering down at me. "Handle my heart with care, not this pussy, baby. I need all of this shit."

Her hair was all over the place. Head dropped back with a light illuminating off of her smooth skin.

She rode this dick like she tamed wild stallions in a past life. Rolling that tight ass pussy up and down, twerking like dollars were being thrown, with her hand around my thick ass neck and a smile on her face. I grabbed her by the throat and flipped her back over. Her legs wrapped around my neck while her titties bounced up and down with the motion. I wasn't a soft nigga by any means but this grip, her eyes, and the tone she moaned my name was going to have me say those three words too soon and pulling this condom off to really give her a reason to stay.

Her moans went silent and her eyes shut. I pulled completely out and slammed back into her. "Give me your voice and your eyes. Don't take that shit from me."

A flood of sound flowed out. She wasn't going to last much longer, and neither was I.

8

Pumae

I had never in my life had anything like that. I couldn't even recall an orgasm that hit that hard. My throat hurt, my center was sore, and the thought of walking didn't even cross my mind, but the sun was coming up. The reality of everything involving Andru and I was hitting me.

"Bitch, did you get fucked into a relationship with a felon who is cleaning drug money for the gang your daddy is a part of?" I whispered to myself sitting up.

I regretted how fast I did. Even my titties were sore. What part of me did he not attack repeatedly? We didn't stop until a few hours ago and even though he wasn't near me, my body still felt him deep inside. I had to think fast. I was either going to lay here and sleep the day away or find a way out of here so I could be at the restaurant on time.

"With what clothes, Pumae? He tore that shit up remember?" I dropped back into the pillows and groaned. "It was some good dick, though."

I rolled over and pulled the covers up to my neck. The tasting for the investors was later on tonight. I had enough time to get more sleep and then slide up out of here. I didn't take into account that Andru was still on prison time and wide awake. He strolled into the room almost thirty minutes later and kissed my face.

"You hungry?" he asked softly against my ear while rubbing my booty.

"You know that answer already," I replied rolling over to look at his face. "You look beautiful in the morning."

He bashfully smiled. "So, do you, Baby. Come eat."

I licked my lips. I could eat but first, it was him I wanted a taste of before I stumbled down the stairs. Ignoring the ache in my muscles, I sat up and tugged at his drawstring. I loved it when dick was ready to go. I was going to consume myself with this shit for as long as I could because why not? If it didn't work at least I had the memory. Taking him fully into my mouth, hearing his hiss caused me to smile. Bobbing, slopping, massaging his balls, I made sure his head was boxing with my tonsils.

Judging from the grunts, the quick strokes in and out of my cheeks, and his toes curling, he wasn't going to last much longer. Of course not, I was giving him my good shit.

"Turn that shit around, push that ass up."

I wasted no time laying on my stomach and spreading my cheeks so he could dive into this pussy full force. Moans turned into screams while I fought the sheets for a grip. Andru's hands found my throat and pulled me up so he could kiss my lips roughly while fucking me like he was on borrowed time.

"Cum for me baby," he growled.

My body was shaking uncontrollably, and a jumble of sound and static fell from my lips. His strokes were getting shorter. Still shaking like a whore in church, I threw my ass back to push him off so I could catch his milk.

"Fuck, Pumae. You ain't leaving."

I wasn't really trying to at this point.

After catching our breath and washing off, he kissed me passionately and placed a light tap on my ass. "Come eat, for real this time."

He grabbed a fresh shirt out of the drawer and handed it to me. I pulled it over my head and followed him down to the kitchen. I was greeted by a full spread and it only forced a bigger smile on my face.

"Before I dig in, I have a question." I pushed my mangled hair out of my face and admired how damn good he looked.

"Ask away." He was busy fixing a plate and kept his eyes on me. I didn't know how he did that, but I was feeling it.

I chuckled nervously and asked, "Did you fuck me into a relationship?"

He laughed. It was probably dick making me hear shit, but his laugh sounded heavenly.

"I told you there was no turning back. After getting a hit of what you got, I ain't with the idea of just letting you get away from me. Call it what you want, relationship, understanding or whatever you want. I ain't trippin' over the title, I know you're mine and you got me without a doubt or a worry. I don't give a damn about a timeline. I wasted seven years of my life. I can't get that back. Everything from this point is done with a purpose. We all in or not. I ain't fucking for a headache or the runaround. I want to build and grow."

"You know you're crazy," I pointed out, enjoying the sight of him shirtless serving me.

"So are you. So, what's up? We crazy together or what?"

I couldn't help but smile. Mom always said it would hit me out of nowhere. It slapped me in the face, and I didn't care how it happened, I just knew it was happening and I wanted to be awake for it.

"Crazy together. But don't play with me, Dru."

"Least of your worries, Baby. I didn't wait this long for something this good to fuck it up. I'm also grown, and I know playing with the puma will get my ass mauled."

"As long as you know."

"You let me know when you pulled a gun on me. You really be shooting niggas?"

"I already answered that," I replied standing up. "Sit down. You took care of me. Let me return the favor."

He put my plate down and sat down. I fixed his food and stood between his legs. I was stripped down, not completely naked, but willing if he opened up the same. I kissed him and took my seat.

"Why don't you drive at night?" he asked, breaking moments of silence thanks to me devouring my food.

"My mother was killed on the bridge at night. She was hit head on by a drunk driver. He lived, of course, you know how the story goes. I don't know...it did something to me and I can't turn it off. I can't drive at night, it messes with me."

"That's why you move like this? Put together, fixing shit, protecting your people?"

I bobbed my head. "You take care of who takes care of you right? Ain't that the code. Monarch's protect each other. All that is cool, but when I'm alone, I'm alone. I don't like that. I can't show it though. People expect something when you're the OG's goddaughter when your father's name shakes people. I just adapted how they moved and made it work for me."

"You don't have to be alone anymore. As long as you got me you'll never be alone, and that's on my life."

I smiled. Whatever euphoria this was shooting through me. "I didn't leave, so have your way."

It was a simple exchange that held weight.

"Why'd you get locked up? I know why but how..."

"I got reckless with my shit. Flashy, arrogant, and sloppy. Plus, I didn't really give a damn about code back then. I thought I could do shit on my own. The same nigga's I gave my ass to kiss were the same nigga's that made sure I was good when I got out. Outside of the family I have, they're my family too."

"Smart man." I smiled. "What's next after Olive and Oak?"

"More spots. Legit spots. And settling. I want a family. I want to come home to some real shit. You down for that?"

"Does family have a timeline?"

"Whenever you're ready."

"Slow up, you got to get past my daddy."

"So, I shouldn't mention the fact you were calling me daddy?" he teased.

"Not unless you want a bullet."

"Like I said, I ain't wasting time. Tell me when and where. We coordinating or what?"

"His birthday is in a week. No need to coordinate."

"Don't knock the coordination, shit is fly."

"Shit isn't."

9

Andru

Part of me was expecting Pumae to shy away from me. You know when that pride sets in and tried to partner with doubt and ruin good shit before it really took off? She couldn't deny it. We had to figure out how to move as a unit in front of King, but everything fell into place quickly. For the first time in years, I felt good. My soul had found its home after searching for it in shit that didn't matter.

Granted I didn't want to be in the gang when I got out, but the gang was more like family. It had its blessings. And she was my biggest blessing thus far.

Seeing how Pumae allowed herself to be free and trust herself with me was beautiful. I couldn't find a flaw, not that I was looking, but even if I did I would find a strength to match it with.

She shined brightly but pushed me into the forefront. King, David, and the rest of the investors loved everything. The restaurant as a whole, the underground operations, and the food to get the cash flowing in and out. Pumae had really busted her ass to pull all of this together.

The sex was top shelf, but I had other ways I wanted to thank her tonight. The tasting was a success last night, but tonight was about celebrating this thing that engulfed us into a freefall.

Being that she still had a hotel suite full of stuff, I was patiently waiting in the lobby for her to come down and bless me with her beauty. Had I gone upstairs, I would have had a fist full of her hair, watching her perfectly round ass bounce up and down.

Reading through a few texts from King about shipments and letting me know that Waters got his stupid ass tied up in a sexual harassment charge. Never liking to see people fall on their faces, but if it meant that his ass was away from me and my lady, I was cool with it. The last message from him was about Pumae.

She didn't come from me, but she's mine. Handle her with care - King

He didn't even need to say it. I knew one wrong step with her, and my ass would wake up looking Whitney Houston in the face wondering how I got there. Replying to his text, the dinging of the elevator briefly caught my attention. Pumae strutted off the elevator like the fierce cat she was. Her long legs shined like she was made out of chocolate and gold dust. I was almost pissed that she wore that short ass skirt and had her titties out. How was I going to pay attention to anything when all I could think of was folding her into a knot.

I stood up and quickly adjusted myself and slid my phone in the jacket. I met her halfway and wrapped my arms around her. "You look too damn good for me to take you in public."

"Mission accomplished," she said with a giggle.

I kissed her and shook my head. "You're trying to make me pack your ass up tonight."

"I took heed to your text. Everything is already packed."

"All I had to do was break you off and you listen?" I teased and took custody of her hand and led her back to the elevator.

"I listen because I want to. Dick just gave me a little push of motivation," she quipped before giving me the side eye. "Where are we going?"

"Back to the room," I said with a straight face.

"I'm not changing," she protested letting go of my hand.

"Girl calm down. The date is on the roof."

She smacked her lips and gently hit my chest. "You play."

"With you for fun, 'cause I like the way you squirm and bite your lip when you're losing control."

The doors of the elevator opened, and I allowed her to switch those hips past me. She leaned against the back of the elevator with an expression that tempted me to stop this ride between floors. But I'd rather have her scream my name above the city.

Joining her, I held her close. I could feel the anticipation of what I had in store for her bounce off of her. Pumae wrapped her arms around my waist and watched as the view from the elevator went from concrete walls to city lights.

"It's beautiful," she murmured, taking in the view of the city in.

"You still thinking about sliding out on me in the middle of the night?" I asked just to be sure. She knew I'd chase her ass wherever she went.

She shook her head no. "Home feels like home again. Thank you for that."

"Ain't no need to thank me. This is what I was designed to do. I just had to go through some hurdles to appreciate this gift.

"You really want to do this, huh?"

Resting my chin in the bend of her neck, I kissed her silky skin. "Ain't never wanted nothing more. All it takes is a step and then another and before you know it, we've discovered a whole new world in each other. I ain't never been soft or putty. But you got me open, willing to do whatever."

She chuckled softly and exhaled. "I'll take care of your heart. Just bare yourself to me, the same way I'm going to do for you."

The elevator doors slid open, exposing the roses and candlelight lit path to the table with dinner. I removed my suit jacket and draped it over her shoulder. Pumae flashed me a thankful look and followed my lead.

I loved how she did that shit. Pumae was a boss, no secret, but in my presence she was soft. A queen. I could tell it was new to her. She hadn't had a king before, which was cool. This would be an experience she would always have.

The rest of the night went beautifully. I found out a lot about her, even the silly shit like her not knowing how to ride a bike or skate. Her childhood was spent with her head in the books. I didn't believe the shit about her being an ugly duckling at all. But the tall kids always got clowned because the short haters were letting their jealousy show.

From the table we went to the railing, sipping wine. Sophisticated shit I swore I'd never do. I wondered how her brandy hued skin mixed with wine. I tasted her neck to see.

"The hotel staff is going to come up here and find you taking all this ass from the back."

I shrugged. "I don't give a damn about them. I was just trying to taste that brandy. But if you want me to stop, I'll get some saran wrap and take this shit to go."

She giggled and turned around. "I didn't say anything about stopping."

She lifted her leg, so her foot was resting on the ledge. Pulling me into a kiss by my tie, her hands worked at my belt buckle. One arm wrapped around her waist to give her extra support, and my free hand ran up and down her thigh. I crept up her skirt only to find she didn't put on any panties. I slipped two fingers inside. Pumae bit down on my lip and hummed in pleasure.

"You think you're slick."

"You said you like playing, so play away."

I played like a fat kid in a candy shop. And so did she. The foreplay was enough for me to fuck her, but I wanted to take my time. I wanted to see how many times I could make her cum with my fingers.

Sloppy kisses, eye contact, and a mission to see who could break the other down faster. We were in for a long night.

10

Pumae

The sun shined on his body just right. My God, he was beautiful. The rays of light highlighted the cuts of his muscles, the healthy beard, and the peaceful expression on his face. I'd never seen anything so beautiful and serene. Nothing like this that wanted to give himself to me and didn't give a damn about money, this gang shit, or another woman. It set butterflies loose all over my being.

After the night we had, he would sleep for another hour at least. As I eased myself out the bed being sure not to wake him, my phone went off. That was daddy's FaceTime ringtone. While I wasn't going to blatantly come out and tell him I was getting my back blown out, I would at least ease him into the idea that I wasn't alone anymore.

I wasn't afraid of daddy. I respected how he wanted certain things presented to him.

Grabbing my thick black robe, I tiptoed out the room onto the balcony. "Good morning, daddy."

"Good morning, daughter," he greeted warmly with a smile plastered on his face. "You look well-rested. King told me the tasting went well. When is the opening?"

"In a few weeks, are you going to be here for it?"

He made a face. "When have I ever missed anything, you've done?"

My daddy hadn't missed shit in my life. I could go on a run in hopes of beating my previous time and he would be following me in the car cheering me along. I was grown and he was embarrassing my ass, but he was proud of me.

"You've never missed a thing I've done. You even went on a few dates with me."

"Hell yeah, so they can understand they can't have you unless they get through me. Speaking of which…"

That was my window. King already told on my ass, I was sure. I rolled my eyes trying to combat the blushing of my cheeks. "Relax he's flying in with me in a few days."

"I let you out of my sight for almost a month and something has happened that fast? You don't even bring home plants, Mae," he joked. He seemed relaxed with the idea of me bringing someone home like it was time for me to stop secluding myself from the world.

"Wellll," I drew out as I admired the peaceful expression on his face. "You and mom always said to never bring home anything I didn't plan on keeping. I didn't want those plants or any of those men"

I could feel his smile beam at me through the screen. I missed him. We'd been partners in crime since mom's transition. It seemed like she made sure to keep us close to one another because she knew we couldn't move on without each other.

"You know all those years of preaching the same sermon to you, I never knew you were listening," he pointed out.

"Daddy, I always listen. I just like doing things my own way from time to time."

He roared in laughter. "From time to time? How about all the damn time. You and your mother."

"Don't do me like that. Mom was one of a kind."

"And you're two of that kind. Where is he?" Dad started moving his head around the screen as if he could see over my shoulder.

"Good morning." Andru didn't even give me the chance to really introduce them, he pulled up behind me fully dressed and nodded in the screen. I was beyond thankful that this man had some good sense about him.

"Pumae," daddy started with a smirk he couldn't hide if he tried. "Go order the man some breakfast and let us talk."

I looked back and forth at both of them. "Y'all can't wait for three days?"

They answered at the same time. "Nah."

As I huffed, Dru helped me to my feet and kissed my face. "Don't worry."

I flashed him a wary look before reluctantly handing my phone over to him. "You make it sound so easy."

He chuckled and responded back in the same hushed tone we'd been exchanging in, "it really is."

Andru took the phone and smiled at me tenderly as I walked backward to the door. He shooed me along but the anxiety of him talking to my daddy without my direction or coaching had me on pins and needles.

"Pumae," dad called.

"Yes, daddy?" I asked like an innocent little girl, not the grown ass woman who was popping pussy a few hours ago.

I stepped inside hoping to stand here and eavesdrop. "Close the door, with you on the other side of it."

I frowned and slid the door shut leaving them to their conversation to talk about me and what would happen to him if he misstepped. It took a great deal of maturity and trust for me to submit to this. It was only because I had become comfortable doing things on my own. No one to answer to, no one to make me communicate, and no one to make sure I was okay.

Sure, I played with the idea of having someone to be and do all of those things for me. For so long, that wasn't my reality.

I watched them engage in a conversation that seemed serious, I didn't move away from the glass door until I saw my dad laugh. Andru looked at me in amusement, got up, and positioned himself where I couldn't see anything. Groaning in frustration of not being in control, I pulled myself away and ordered breakfast.

I still tried to strain my ears to listen while I talked to the kitchen. From Andru's body language it seemed like everything was okay. Cordial enough for me to leave it alone and take a shower. For a split second, I was considering cutting this shit right now. Then, I saw Dru's reassuring look in my head and I heard his heavy baritone rumble against my flesh, *you can't make me leave you.*

My anxiety settled and I pulled myself together. I focused fully on the task at hand, detangle my hair, wash these thick tresses, and if time permitted, blow dry it enough not to be wrestling with it later. Finally wrapping up my shower, I walked out into the room and threw his button-up over my arms. Andru was sitting on the balcony with his shirt off arranging the plates. When I found out he ran the kitchen in prison, I let him live about being up before the sun, cooking every morning.

"You know I like my food with a view," I announced, flipping my curls out of my face.

He looked up at me and froze for a moment. "Wow."

"What?" My brows dipped.

"I like that."

I scoffed. "I look like a poodle."

"Bring your fine ass over here."

My feet pranced over to him before my brain could register. I pranced right into his arms and kissed the center of his chest. "You good?"

"I'm great. Your pops is cool."

"I almost pulled the plug on this. If daddy doesn't like you then…"

"Pops and I would just have to have an understanding about this. His daughter, but my lady. Shit is simple."

"And is that how you told him that? I snatched up your daughter, she's mine now?"

"Nah, do you know who your pops is?" he quizzed.

"I know exactly who he is."

"Then you know your pops already knew who I was and what I was about before we even crossed paths. We have an understanding. He wants you to be happy and I want to live. A simple exchange."

Playfully, I scoffed and stepped away from him. "Boy, you talk shit."

He looked over his shoulder before looking me up and down. "When did we have a son?"

My face twisted a little. "What?"

"Ain't shit about me a boy, Baby," he grumbled.

My eyes took sport in watching his brows dipped when he was about to dig into his shit talking bag. I was tempted to make him do this all day so he could break it down later.

"I don't talk shit, Baby. You should know that. I mean what I say and every move I make mirrors that. You know I know what I want. You know what you want. Stop trying to downplay that shit, eat up so I can take your pretty ass home."

11

Andru

Pumae had only been in my spot for three days and it already felt like home. Although having her around took some adjusting to, I didn't mind it. I loved this shit if we were real about it. She had her way of doing things and I had my conditioned way about shit.

For instance, she had a habit of lying her toothbrush by the sink, I wanted them upright in the cup. She studied me with those beautiful eyes, taking amusement with how I twisted my face and picked up her toothbrush and dropped it in the cup. There was a slick ass grin spreading across her lips. "Let's call it even. You forget to put the seat down, I don't put that toothbrush back."

I laughed to myself and nodded. "If this is the only disagreement we're having, I'm cool with it."

Pumae ran her hands through her thick curls and managed to pull them into a ponytail. "Are you ready for this weekend?"

"Born ready," I shot back confidently.

"You know there isn't any fuckin' in daddy's house," she shared glancing over at me.

"What about outside?" I asked. "I can control myself, but dammit you're addictive."

She snickered and threw the final things she needed this weekend in her bag. "I'm going to have to ration this."

"Hell nah."

Pumae hummed to herself. She was trying to keep her comment to herself, but she knew I needed her voice to grace my ears. I needed her words.

"Say it, Baby," I urged.

"I can't have you getting tired of it or me."

I snorted in laughter and walked out of the bathroom. Gathering her bags, I stopped a few inches short of her and kissed her supple lips. "That ain't ever going to happen. Watch and see."

The smile erased the worry on her face. Placing a light tap to her thigh I kissed her again. "Let's go."

After half a day of traveling, we were finally at her pops compound. The OG's moved differently from the rest of us. I couldn't front, this shit was enticing. Just from the glimpse of security walking around in suits, guns and organization made me understand why Pumae moved around the way she did. She'd been chauffeured around in bulletproof Maybach's, Bentley's and Rolls Royce's. With all of this at her fingertips, you could tell she was kept but she didn't move like hard work was beneath her.

She had layers to her. Pops used to tell me if you wanted to know what kind of woman you had to look at the stock she came from. Yasir Jones wasn't nothing to play with and he took his safety and his daughter's seriously.

"Welcome to my home away from home," Pumae muttered as she climbed out the truck.

The front door opened and Pumae took off in a full sprint to her pops who was just as tall as I was. They collided into one another and embraced like she'd been off at war. It was no secret they loved each other. They were each other's support. Yasir was a proud man, especially when it came to her. He wasn't going to hand her over to any nigga with a silver tongue.

My hands gripped the straps of the three bags she packed for three days. A suit bag because apparently I couldn't just carry my shit through the airport, a bag for her heels, I was going to make sure she modeled at least three pairs for me, and another bag full of other shit.

Yasir finished fawning over his daughter and met me halfway. "She doesn't carry bags. I tried breaking her out of that habit, it never worked."

I chuckled softly. "She doesn't have to do that if I'm around."

He sized me up then extended his hand. "Nice to meet you in person. Phone calls from prison and FaceTime calls don't give you the essence."

"They don't but character always precedes everything else," I replied back looking up briefly to see that

Pumae had disappeared inside of the house. I shook his hand with my free hand and nodded.

"Chauncey," Yasir waved one of the security guards over and pointed to the bags. "Take these to their room please."

Chauncey took the bags from me and strolled into the house. Once we were alone, Yasir started up again. "When your pops told me to look out for you before he passed, I didn't think that you'd fuse into my family the way you've done."

I didn't say anything. I needed to see where he was going before I spoke up.

"We're not just entrusting you with our money and our product, we are entrusting you with a gem. One of a kind and has been through enough heartbreak to last her a lifetime. I'm trusting you with my daughter. If you cannot handle that responsibility the car is waiting to take you back to the airport."

He stopped walking, put his hands in his pockets, and waited on my answer. Crazy shit was how the Monarch's looked out for my family while I was away and put me into a position after getting out. They already welcomed me in, but this step wasn't one I was planning on taking.

"I didn't even know I needed Pumae," I started, trying to hold face and ward off any emotions that were reserved for her only. "Not until she walked in and filled a space that I was cool with being empty. I was fine paying off my pops debt with my head held down under the radar. I was fine with working my debt off with y'all. What I won't be okay with is walking away from her. Pumae is your daughter, and I appreciate everything you and your late wife poured into her. She's also my wife. I know that without a doubt. She was made for me. And with your blessing, I'd like to continue to build with her."

"And if I say no…"

"Then you and I will have to reach an understanding because I won't let her get away from me, and I'm not leaving."

Yasir scoffed, scowled for a moment before grinning. "Damn it, I thought I liked you before!"

Shaking my hand and pulling into a half hug, he embraced me before he let me go. "King was right about you. You got heart. I respect that shit. And I've never seen my daughter shine the way she has. Protect her light."

"With my life."

Now that we'd gotten the conversation out of the way I had to deal with another reality. Pumae was used to finer things and whereas I had ends, I didn't have the ends her pops had. I watched how everything moved from the time we arrived until the time the cake came out at the party. I wasn't that nigga who was going to be pushing hundred thousand dollar cars around the city for the hell of it.

Yes, I was going to provide. Yes, I was going to shower her in love and things that meant something, but I wasn't comfortable drawing attention to myself like this. Going back to prison due to a lifestyle addiction was not a factor I was willing to compromise with.

Slipping out of the party, I strolled down to the pond. There were barely people out here. I didn't want to talk, I just needed to clear my head and lose track of the time in my thoughts. However, I meant to slip back in before Pumae noticed I was gone.

"There you are," her smooth voice graced my ears and every nerve ending in my body sparked with attention.

Pumae wrapped her arms around my torso and rested her head in the center of my back. "Why'd you leave?"

"I just needed some air," I muttered.

I could have really been in my head about this shit. But I couldn't ignore it and fall back into my old ways of doing things. She unwrapped her arms and positioned herself in front of me so she could see my face.

"You're going to have to try that again. Talk to me."

I inhaled sharply and looked away. "I'm cool."

"Andru Towns. That's not going to work for me. I need your voice. You're going to have to use your words when you're talking to me." She used my words against me. "What's going on?"

"Do you want this?" I finally looked down at her. "The parties and the cars and flashy ass gangsta life?"

"What are we, if we're not gangsters?" she quizzed. The expression on her face only made my chest ache more. I could peer down into her eyes and see my entire life, but one misstep and it was all gone.

"Regular ass people who can live normally without looking over our shoulder. All this shit got me caught up the first time. I don't want to fall back into my old ways."

She shrugged, flipped her hair over her shoulder, and said, "then don't. I'm not forcing this on you. I don't know what this is about, but I know what you stand for and what *you're* about. I'm not going to put you in a position to go back. I don't care about the glitz and glam of this shit. I live in a three-bedroom house in a modest neighborhood."

Pumae tilted her head to make sure she still had my attention. "Baby, if I wanted this shit, I would have created it for myself. I am looking at what I want. Stability - the house, the kids, the dog, and maybe that god awful white picket fence you want. This shit has hit us like a freight train but we're in it. I don't even think if we tried to walk away we could. Get out of your head, please."

I washed my hand over my face and hissed. "Shit. Did you just put me back in my place?"

"I did. Gently of course, because I know you like being handled with care." She took a deep sigh while wrapping her soft hands in mine. "Baby it's us. No one is going to understand this, but us. And I'm standing here. I can't let my fears run me off and neither can you."

I pulled her into my body and took possession of her lips.

"You a wonder," I muttered.

"I know I am."

Falling off of my square didn't happen often but the way she put me back on was impeccable. We stood by the water tonguing each other down without a care in the world. I was ready to ease up off of her, collect myself and take her back inside the party, but she had other plans.

"You said no fucking in your pop's spot."

"We aren't in his spot." Pumae was assertive and I loved that shit. The facets to her personality that kept me on my toes - kept my sharp.

Falling captive to her will, I waited in anticipation of what she was going to do. Pumae had me spellbound since my eyes landed on all five foot eleven inches of her thick copper-toned body. My being entrusted itself with her.

My eyes stayed on her slick ass grin while my feet walked backward under her command. Just when she had me where she wanted me, she pushed me down onto the bench a few feet away.

It wasn't long before my dick was buried inside of her welcoming walls and she rode me reverse cowgirl. Pumae's pants and soft moans were beautifully enticing sweeping away every fear I had conjured up. My hands were tightly entangled in hers pressing against her breast through the cream dress she wore.

A soft glance pulled my eyes to hers as the softest plea fell from her lips. "Please don't ever look for another reason to leave me."

Although we were surrounded by nature and our damn near uncontrollable need for each other, I heard her loud and clear.

When we returned to the party, it was livelier than before. Cigar smoke, dark liquor, and champagne replaced the dessert wines and cakes I left behind. With so much activity and noise the only thing I felt, smelled, and saw was Pumae. Gentle in all of her power to ground me and ease the anxiety.

As she lit my cigar and stroked my arm she blessed me with a wink. "I got you."

12

Pumae

My head was pounding. It had a damn percussion beat of its own. Any other time I would have appreciated a good beat, but this was outright tortuous. The night before was a blur. How I made it out of the party, washed, hair tied, and into the bed was a mystery that Dru could solve for me. But I was in too much pain to ask.

I couldn't pinpoint the last time I was this hungover. Normally, I was good at holding my liquor. It was probably the shots I took with daddy and my uncles. They were the cause of this road of destruction I walked down.

The last day was spent between the bed and the bathroom. The only person in the house who was well enough to function was Dru. He kept his consumption to a minimum. The man had his ways about control, and I was thankful for it. We all couldn't be on our ass regretting the decision we made in the spirit of celebrating daddy's fiftieth.

Although Dru had been a wonderful caretaker, his patience was wearing thin with my slothfulness. We were set to be at church with his mother and sister in an hour and I'd barely made it out of the bed. We even flew back late last night so we could be on time.

"Why are you looking at me with that look that you're looking at me with?" I questioned playfully, dragging myself to the bathroom.

Andru had been up for hours because he was conditioned. "You know just as important as it was for me to meet your father it is equally as important for us to be on time for service."

Since he had a valid point I put some pep into my step. Quickly showering and stumbling out to brush my teeth, I was met at the vanity with Excedrin and a bottle of water.

"Drink the whole thing, Baby," he directed from the closet.

"Are you willing to tell your mother the reason we were late?" I quizzed throwing a couple of pills into my mouth.

"Not by a long shot," he quickly replied followed with a soft laugh.

Leaving it alone for now, I did my make-up - enough to open my eyes and make me look lively without looking like a whore. I pulled my hair into a high ponytail and jumped into my cream high waisted skirt. As I buttoned the cream blouse, Andru knelt at my feet and helped me into my heels.

"Why must you look good in everything?" he grunted gently running his hand up my calf.

I licked my lip and toyed with the idea of getting a quickie in. One enticing touch of his hand had me ready to go. How was I going to sit through a sermon with my homegirl purring?

"You are not about to get me hot and bothered before we walk into the house of the Lord. Stop it."

He chuckled and stood up. "You're right. If we are any later than we are now, she's going to tear my ass up."

"As long as it's you and not me." I took a deep breath and gathered my emotions. "You know I haven't been on the inside of that church since my mother's funeral?"

Andru didn't hesitate pulling me into his arms to kiss my face. He then pulled away and gave me a soft glare and a wink. "I got you."

Grabbing my long jacket off the end of the bed and my purse, I took a deep breath and followed him out of the house. You would have thought he was running from the law the way he was weaving in and out of traffic to get to Mount Olive AME.

It was a megachurch that sat at the end of Olive Boulevard, right at the end of sinners' row. Clubs, bars, and a few other places were under its cast of golden light from the giant cross that sat at the top of the building. It was almost like it drew all the sinners right to it. The pews were full every Sunday with the elite of Ganton Hills, along with the scum.

Andru parked the Range in the closest spot to the entrance of the church and led me in.

"The Lord knows what we did between the hours of two and four,"' I mumbled following the usher to our seats, in the front of the church.

He tried his best to hide his laughter. "He forgives sinners like us, doesn't he?"

"That's what I heard, but we're about to find out," I whispered back ignoring all the eyes on us as we took this incredibly long walk to the front where his mother and sister sat. "We might get struck by lightning."

"All the sinners in here better get hit with us," he replied as we finally reached the front.

Worship was still in full force, thank God. I would have hated to walk in here as the pastor was addressing his wayward flock.

Andru waved at his sister and mother while letting me in the pew first. Unsure of how they were going to receive me, they both pulled me into a welcoming hug.

"My God, you are beautiful," his mother muttered looking me over.

"He might've paid her mom," his sister teased.

Andru rolled his eyes, picked up his niece, and greeted the two leading women in his life. "I'm in church, I'm not going to act a fool in here. But you just wait."

Him and his sister shared a looked before laughing and turning their attention back to the praise team.

A brief glance at Andru holding his niece and swaying to the music made my heart flutter. And then joy sparked through my spirit. He was mine. As service continued, Andru held my hand, caressed my knuckles, and met my anxious spirit with peace.

"I told you I had you," he whispered in my ear after service was over.

We stood huddled in the front of the church a few feet away from his mother, the pastor, and the first lady who chatted amongst themselves.

"So, Andru," his sister started up. "How did you manage to snag a beauty like..."

"Pumae," I answered.

"Divine intervention," Andru spoke up.

She smirked. "And exotic. I'm Ryan. His older sister, sometimes he forgets who the oldest is."

Andru rolled his eyes and blew kisses at his niece. "You should start acting your age then, Ryan."

She cut him a look of her own before focusing on me fully. "What do you do, Pumae?"

"I'm a restaurant planner," I confidently answered.

She nodded again and their mother entered the huddle. "Ryan, leave the girl alone. Andru you're coming over for dinner right?"

"We're going to follow y'all to the house," he answered.

Being that I was beyond ready to eat, I didn't object at all. I could handle both of them on my own. Ryan was trying to size me up to see if I was a good fit for her brother while his mother was going to silently watch me and then form her opinion. Either way, I was ready. And like Andru, if they didn't like me, we would just have to come to an understanding.

Halfway through dinner and small talk, his mother looked up at us and opened her line of questioning. "Are you equipped to take care of my son?"

Dapping the corners of my mouth with the napkin, I met her eye contact. "I am, through his anxiousness, his conditioning, and his assertiveness. Dru requires a certain tone and touch, an ability that came naturally."

"Naturally, after a month?" Ryan chimed in.

"Time is irrelevant. We -"

"I got this one, Baby," he said, sitting up. "Ryan, a man knows who he wants within minutes of meeting a woman. He doesn't waste time or linger or drag her along for a ride. He makes his stance known and he will move earth to get and keep what is his. I didn't need years to tell me that she was made for me. I knew, and I made the necessary arrangements to fuse my life with hers."

"You just knew?" his mom asked with a smile.

"I just knew."

"You didn't have to read me like that, Dru," Ryan huffed, crossing her arms.

"I'm not. I'm just telling you what's real. I know what I stumbled into is real. She knew what I needed without me saying a word. I spent seven years away from everything praying that when I was finally free everything I wanted and needed would rain down on me. I don't have any more time to waste, I have to love right now with all that I have."

We all looked at him with the same expression. Andru turned to me and swiped my chin. "Don't act like you don't know what this is, Baby."

I tucked my lip between my teeth.

"Just tell me you're staying...I need you here with me."

For twenty seconds everything faded but him. "I'll stay."

"Would you look at this," his mom said, clasping her hands together. "I got my son back and a potential daughter in law. You're not pregnant are you?"

"Nah, she ain't ...yet."

"Yet?!" Ryan and I said together.

"I said what I said."

13

Andru

The restaurant was packed from the private dining rooms where our families had joined to celebrate the tireless work and planning that went into opening my pops' spot back up. Debt aside, I was proud of this. I was proud to hold a beacon to his legacy. I'm sure if he were here, we'd be lighting cigars and sharing jokes. I missed him, but I felt his spirit.

Walking into the private dining room to see Pumae, my mother, and Ryan laughing and passing dishes, I smiled. Yasir, King, and David sat on the other side of the room just as happy as everyone else. There hadn't been a complaint from anyone about anything. We were on our way, and with Pumae by my side, my success was limitless.

I leaned over and kissed her exposed shoulder. "How is everything?"

"So good, but you knew that." She beamed. "When are you going to sit down and eat?"

"When we close," I answered. "Don't eat too much. I need you to keep me company."

She laughed and shook her head. "This dress is telling, I am looking forward to really eating."

I chuckled and stood up as the waitress bought the chilled bottles of champagne in. I waited until everyone had theirs before strolling to the front of the room to make a toast.

"I want to thank all of you. Everyone in this room has been a facilitator in my transition and the continuation of my family's legacy - of our family's legacy. Mom, Ryan, I would be remiss not to give you your flowers because I'm not shit without y'all. Pops, your stubbornness is unmatched but your vision for your family, especially your little boy, was clear. The gatekeepers, the monarchy - thank you for all this shit…"

The trio raised their glasses and nodded graciously.

"There's someone else who really needs more than a thank you, though. When I walked into this building almost two months ago, I had no idea how we were going to clean it up and open. I didn't know how I was going to continue this legacy but with assertion, a .45 Beretta, and an unmatched work ethic, Pumae got the job done. But she's much more than a force to be reckoned with. Much more than a beautiful woman with a crazy ass dedication to be her best and make sure everything she touches is gold. She's my heart."

Pumae gave me a warning glare with the smile she was trying to hide. "Please, stop," she mouthed.

"Baby, come up here real quick."

She rose from her seat and floated over to me. Taking her place at my side, she smiled up at me. I turned to take her hand in mine and kiss her knuckles. "No one told me I was going to fall in love on the corner of Olive and Oak three weeks removed from prison. No one told me that in two months I would be so attached to everything you are that I wouldn't stand to be out of your presence and your covering. You have shifted my world while filling it to the brim. Your touch has been the most electrifying and settling pulse I've ever experienced. Ain't no secret that I love you. Ain't no secret that I'm trying to spend my forever with you. I just want to make it official…"

Lowering myself down to one knee and pulling the ring box from my pocket, I open the custom made diamond ring from The Diamond Jeweler. "You love me, Pumae Jones?"

"Like crazy."

"Let's get married, then."

She giggled and shook her head. "Let's get married."

L et the adventure begin. Welcome to Ganton Hills.

ABOUT THE AUTHOR

Hailing from the illustrious South Carolina State University, Aubreé Pynn is a self-proclaimed "lover of love!" With forty-two titles published under her pen, she has no plans of slowing down. Her mission: cultivating enticing tales centering Black love. Her hope: you'll buckle up and enjoy the ride.

ALSO BY AUBREE PYNN

Urban Romance

Dope Boys: Anything for the Throne

Her Goon, His Eden

Run From Me

Contemporary Romance

Everything is love

My Love For You: The Collection

Love 101

Color Me, You

Because Love Said So

Say He'll Be My Valentine

Impulsive Emotion

The Last Christmas

Get Me Back

Edible Arrangements

Summer Love

Wants and Needs

Poetry

Coldest Summer Ever

SumWhereOvaRainbows

Queendom

The Essence of You

Stranger Things

Series

The Way you Lie 1-2

All to Myself 1-2

Love the Series 1-4

Indigo Haze 1-4

Forbidden lust series 1-4

Collaborations

One Last Chance Series